Alligators and Others All Year Long!

A Book of Months

Crescent Dragonwagon
illustrated by Jose Aruego
and Ariane Dewey

Macmillan Publishing Company   New York
Maxwell Macmillan Canada   Toronto
Maxwell Macmillan International   New York   Oxford   Singapore   Sydney

For Juan—J.A. and A.D.

First edition. Printed in Hong Kong by South China Printing Company (1988) Ltd. The text of this book is set in 16 pt. Veljovic Book. The illustrations are rendered in pen-and-ink and gouache.   10 9 8 7 6 5 4 3 2 1

Library of Congress Cataloging-in-Publication Data. Dragonwagon, Crescent. Alligators and others all year long! : a book of months / Crescent Dragonwagon ; illustrated by Jose Aruego and Ariane Dewey. — 1st ed.   p.   cm. Summary: A collection of animals celebrate the months of the year, one by one, in poetry. ISBN 0-02-733091-5 1. Months—Juvenile poetry. 2. Animals—Juvenile poetry. 3. Children's poetry, American. [1. Months—Poetry. 2. Animals—Poetry. 3. American poetry—Collections.] I. Aruego, Jose, ill. II. Dewey, Ariane, ill. III. Title.   PS3554.R183A79 1993   811'.54—dc20   91-2831

For Crow Johnson,

with love and gray braids, a fiddle and a drum — C.D.

One year is old,
one year is new.
Oh full, long year
for me and you!

Twelve months,
like presents, in a row—
with twelve wrapped up,
and twelve to go.

Oh year of friends and holidays,
of clouded skies, of suns that blaze,
of food and family, home and cheer—
oh precious, full, surprising year!

Call it a circle,
call it a ring.
Twelve months to fill
with everything!

...and then begin again.

January

It starts this month
in icy white.
It starts—
twelve months of pure delight!

We'll invite Cat,
for soup and skating.
It's time to start
the celebrating!
        in January.

February

In February,
Fox will find
it's hard to address
Valentines.

The cards are pink,
with hearts and flowers,
but writing names out
can take *hours*.

So Fox forgoes
the enveloping,
delivering by
four Fox-feet loping
        in February

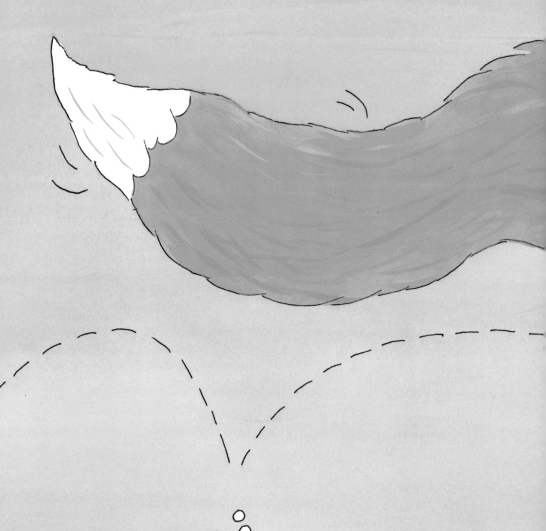

March

In March, a Moose
meanders hills
in search of yellow
daffodils.

And when she finds
a charming bunch,
she bites their heads off
for her lunch.

And when she's more
than had her fill,
she might bring one more daffodil
back to a friend,
       in March.

April

In April,
Alligators go
from muddy mud
and wet below

to sun themselves,
above, on logs
along the very
choicest bogs.

Their hibernation's
done and through;
it's time to feast
—on me and you?
        in April.

May

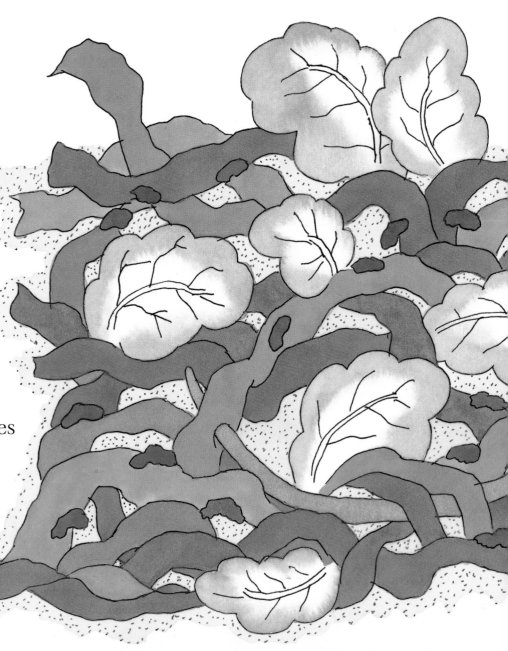

A Mouse might make
a mess in May,
inspired on
a sunny day:

"I'll shred up something
for a nest,
blue tissue paper's
always best—

but lint is nice,
and sawdust, too,
and moss, and cabbage leaves
will do just right for me,
    in May."

June

Jaguar plays
a jazzy tune,
his trumpet glistening
in June.

And all the frogs
sing, "croate, croate, croate,"
in harmony
on every note.

The lizards click,
the fish flash fins,
the dizzy ducklings
get the spins
in June.

July

July's Seagulls
salute the flag,
then open up
the picnic bag

for sandwiches,
but then they spy
a very large
blueberry pie.

They squawk with greed,
then Old Gull speaks:
"We'll just divide it,
with our beaks."
                in July.

August

In August, Dragonfly
will float
above the Lotus Castle
moat.

Her wings
are iridescent gauze.
"Why are your wings so blue?"
"Because—

Because they're cool,
and light as air,
because they're mine,
because they're there."
            in August.

September

In September,
Chick's afraid
to go into
the second grade.

But Hen says, "Look,
some bright new clothes,
are all you need—
a mother knows."

And sure enough,
in feathers fine,
Chick soon is leading
recess line
      in September.

October

Swan's goal is really
very clear:
to carve the pumpkin
of the year.

A pumpkin bigger
than a house,
which he'll show off
to Chick and Mouse.

A pumpkin that will
win a prize,
with fang-y teeth,
and rolling eyes.

An orange
jack-o'-lantern king;
Swan carves so long
he sprains his wing!
And friends brings treats, in October.

November

Thanksgiving and
the Pigs rejoice—
so many pies!
And so much choice!

Peach and apple,
cherry, ample
mincemeat, pumpkin—
just a sample,

crumb or nibble
of each kind,
our gracious hostess
will not mind
        in November.

December

In December,
we can see
it's time to get
a Christmas tree

and light it up,
with strings of lights,
to brighten dark
December nights.

And presents for our friends,
our dears,
who made this best
of all the years:
      A singing song December.

The Presents

January
skates
for Cat

February
mail pouch
for Fox

March
daffodil catsup
for Moose

April
mud buckets
for the Alligators

May
art supplies
for Mouse

June
trumpet polish
for Jaguar

July
picnic basket
for the Seagulls

August
blue bow
for Dragonfly

September
book bag
for Chick

October
pumpkin-carving
tools for Swan

November
large plates
for the Pigs

And a
December song
for everyone!

The December Song for Everyone

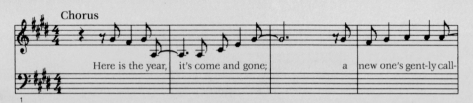

Chorus

Here is the year, it's come and gone; a new one's gent-ly call-

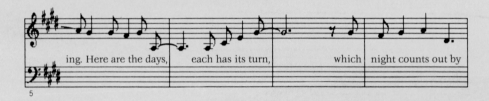

ing. Here are the days, each has its turn, which night counts out by

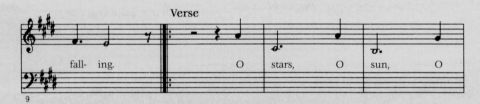

Verse

fall- ing. O stars, O sun, O

rains, O snows O kiss-e-s and yes-se-s and

hu--gs and no's.

O days with friends
to joke and bake
O red balloons
and birthday cake.

Chorus

O days alone,
to think and read,
O gardens planted
with flower seed.

Chorus

O friends O months
O golden days
O every day's
a holiday!

Chorus